JASON STRANGE

STRAYS

Cover art by Alberto Dal Lago

Interior art by Nelson Evergreen

STONE ARCH BOOKS
a capstone imprint

Jason Strange is published by Stone Arch Books
A Capstone Imprint
1710 Roe Crest Dr.
North Mankato, Minnesota 56003
www.capstonepub.com

Copyright © 2012 by Stone Arch Books

Cataloging-in-Publication Data is available at the Library of Congress website.

ISBN: 978-1-4342-3295-3 (library binding)
ISBN: 978-1-4342-3883-2 (paperback)

Summary: When fourteen-year-old Quentin's bike breaks down in the strange town of Ravens Pass, he and his friend Reese find themselves surrounded by feral cats--is this an attack or something else?

Art Director: Kay Fraser
Graphic Designer: Hilary Wacholz
Production Specialist: Michelle Biedscheid

Photo credits:
Shutterstock: Nikita Rogul (handcuffs, p. 2); Stephen Mulcahey (police badge, p. 2); B&T Media Group (blank badge, p. 2); Picsfive (coffee stain, pp. 2, 5, 12, 17, 24, 30, 42, 48, 57); Andy Dean Photography (paper, pen, coffee, pp. 2, 66); osov (blank notes, p. 1); Thomas M Perkins (folder with blank paper, pp. 66, 67); M.E. Mulder (black electrical tape, pp. 69, 70, 71)

Printed in the United States of America in Stevens Point, Wisconsin.
102011   006404WZS12

TABLE OF CONTENTS

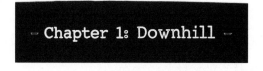

— Chapter 1: Downhill —

Quentin Sparks leaned over the handlebars of his road bike. His feet stopped spinning the pedals as he let himself coast down a steep, winding hill.

His friend Reese hadn't been far behind him when they'd started the climb. Now, though, Reese was still climbing, while Quentin was enjoying the high speed of a wicked descent.

The wind rushed over Quentin's face and through his hair, cooling him after a long day of riding. He and Reese had been on their bikes since early that morning. They'd left their hometown by the route they always took, but for the ride home, Reese had suggested something new.

"I've heard about a great ride back," Reese had said at a rest stop. "The hills are supposed to be huge."

Quentin loved a hilly ride, so he was happy to agree. As he flew down the hill now, he saw a small town spread out before him at the bottom. Quentin stopped and turned just before the hill flattened out and became the town's Main Street.

Quentin watched Reese cruise down from the top of the hill toward him.

Quentin waved to let Reese know he should stop.

"What's up?" Reese said as he skidded to a halt next to his friend. "Some ride, huh?"

Quentin smiled and nodded. "Excellent," he agreed. Then he looked over his shoulder at the little town behind him. "Have you ever heard of this place?"

A small sign stood next to the road. It read, "Welcome to Ravens Pass." Although it was spring and the grass all around was healthy and green, the wild flowers growing at the base of the sign were black and wilting.

Reese shook his head. "Nope," he said. "When Jake told me about this route, he didn't mention any town."

"Maybe we went the wrong way," Quentin said.

Reese frowned. "No way am I going back up that hill," he said. "I'm sure we're heading in the right direction. Let's just cut through town. It'll take like forty-five seconds, tops."

Quentin nodded. "Okay, let's go," he said.

The boys started through town. There were a few cars parked on Main Street, and one little pizza place was open, but they didn't see any other people.

"Sure is quiet here," Reese called out to Quentin as they rode through town. "Let's get some pizza. I'm starving."

Quentin nodded. "Okay," he said. He reached down for his water bottle.

As Quentin tilted back his head and brought the bottle to his mouth, Reese shouted, "Quentin, look out!"

A lean black cat darted in front of his bike. Quentin nearly dropped his water as he struggled to swerve. The cat seemed to stare right at him.

Its eyes shone gold and yellow as it opened its mouth and hissed. Quentin skidded and screeched along the pavement, trying to keep his bike steady.

Quentin's rear wheel spun out on some loose gravel. He flew from the bike and landed hard on the pavement.

- Chapter 2: Ghost Town -

Quentin groaned as he struggled to his feet.

"Are you okay?" Reese said. He stopped his bike, then ran to his friend's side. "You're bleeding."

Quentin looked at his left elbow and knee. Both were scraped up and dirty. "It's not too bad," he said. "I have a first-aid kit in my bike bag."

Reese ran to Quentin's bike to get the kit.

"Uh-oh," Reese said. "Look at your bike, Q."

Quentin looked up. His bike hadn't escaped the fall with just a few dings, like he had. It had slid into a lamppost, front wheel first. The rim was bent badly.

"I bet there isn't even a bike shop in this tiny town," Quentin said. He got up to get a closer look at the wheel. "I can't ride home on this."

Reese sighed. "What was with that cat, anyway?" he asked.

Quentin shook his head. "I have no idea," he said. "It came right at me."

"Let's look around," Reese said. "Maybe there's a bike shop."

Quentin looked at his bike and sighed. "I guess I don't have a choice," he said.

Reese smiled. "Cheer up," he said. "If we can find a bike shop, we can get that pizza while your bike's getting fixed."

The boys started walking their bikes along Main Street. Before long, Reese spotted the logo of a bicycle in a storefront window. "Over there," he said, pointing at it.

Quentin squinted. "It looks kinda dark inside," he said.

Reese shrugged. "We don't have any other options," he said. "Let's go check it out."

The boys walked toward the shop. It was closed, and all the lights were off. Quentin put his face to the window, hoping someone might be inside. He could see the repairs section at the back. A huge selection of bicycle rims was hanging on the walls.

Quentin sighed. "So close, yet so far," he said.

Reese saw that a thick layer of dust covered nearly everything in the shop. "Weird," Reese said. "It looks like they don't get a lot of business."

"You're right," Quentin said. He glanced around the empty town. It was only in the late afternoon, but all of the stores and shops he could see had *CLOSED* signs hanging on their doors.

Where is everybody? Quentin wondered.

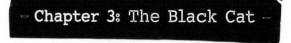

Chapter 3: The Black Cat

"It looks like I'm going to have to call my parents," Quentin said. He dropped to the sidewalk and sat down on the curb.

"Great," Reese said. "Your mom will never let you go on a full-day ride again."

Reese noticed something on the ground beneath his feet. "What's that?" he asked, lifting his foot.

Quentin bent over and picked up a small sheet of paper.

"In emergencies," he read aloud, "see Carol in the Pizza Shop."

"Who's Carol?" Reese said.

"I guess she must own that pizza place you wanted to go to," Quentin said. "Let's head over there. We might not have to call my parents after all!"

With a new sense of hope, the boys walked their bikes back up Main Street. As the pizza shop came into view, Quentin could see through the big front window. A woman was standing behind the counter, reading a magazine. Her hair was dark and long, and she had a friendly smile on her face.

"That must be Carol," Quentin said. He glanced at the horizon. The sun was getting low. "Let's hurry. It's getting late."

The woman looked up at them through the double glass doors as they got close. But when Quentin reached for the handle, a skinny black cat bounded in front of them. It stood between them and the front of the shop.

"It's the same cat," Quentin said, taking a step back.

It was obviously a stray. Its fur was matted and tangled. The cat looked like it had been in its fair share of cat-fights. The cat stared right at Quentin. "What's wrong with that thing?" he said.

Reese rolled his eyes. "Come on," he said. "It's just a cat."

"Just a cat?" Quentin snapped. "The thing is evil! It tried to kill me, and it wrecked my front wheel!"

"Don't be ridiculous," Reese said. "It's just a little lonely, that's all."

Reese stepped slowly toward the cat and leaned down. He put out his open hand and said, "Nice kitty. That's a good kitty."

The cat drew back against the pizzeria door. It arched its back, ruffled its fur, and let out a sharp hiss.

The cat swiped its claws at Reese, but he quickly jerked his hand away. "Yikes," he said. "Maybe it *is* a little evil."

Inside, the woman at the counter was watching the two boys. She was still smiling, and now she was waving at them, as if to say, "Come on in."

"Okay," Quentin said. "I can do this. It's just a stupid cat."

Quentin took a deep breath.

Then he took a slow step toward the shop. His foot came down on the pavement with a loud thud as he tried to scare the cat away. Instead, the cat lunged at him, hissing in midair.

Quentin threw his arms up to cover his face. The cat scratched his cheek as it flew past, drawing blood.

The cat landed next to him and hissed. "Get it away from me!" Quentin shouted. He covered the cuts on his face with his hand as the cat stalked toward him for another attack.

Reese ran over and knocked the cat away. It spun and snarled, baring its pointy little teeth at Reese.

Quentin pointed behind Reese. "Look out!" he shouted.

Reese turned. Two more street cats were slinking toward him. One was orange and mangy, and the other was gray. Both were dirty, and their coats were tangled. The cats pounced, scratching at the boys' arms and tearing at their clothes.

The cats gathered together in front of the double doors to the pizza place. All three looked ready to attack. The boys tensed, preparing themselves to fight — or run.

"They're trying to stop us from going in," Quentin said.

"They're definitely weird, but they're just stray cats," Reese insisted. "We have to get inside to get your bike fixed, right? Besides, the pizza smells great, and I'm starving."

Just then, two more cats prowled toward the boys from the left.

Quentin spotted them and shook his head. "We have to get out of here," he said. "Let's leave for a few minutes, then come back when they're gone."

Suddenly, the two prowling cats dashed at the boys.

"Run!" Reese said. They dropped their bikes and bolted.

Chapter 4: Cat Walk

"Are they gone?" Quentin asked.

The boys were leaning against a brick wall, just around the corner from the pizza place. Reese slowly peeked around to see if it was safe.

"Nope," he said. "Still there. Oh, wait a minute . . ."

"What?" Quentin asked. He got up and peeked around the corner too.

When Carol came out of the shop, the cats slowly moved away from the door and hissed.

"They're not attacking her," Reese said. "She's locking up!"

"Oh no!" Quentin said. "We have to stop her. I need her to fix my bike, or we'll be stuck here."

Reese nodded. "Let's go, quick," he said.

But the moment they turned the corner, the cats were blocking them. They formed a line of fur and claws that the boys couldn't get past.

Quentin watched Carol unlock the door of a small green car. She climbed inside. "Great," he said. "She's in her car. We'll never catch up to her now."

When the little green car had driven off, the cats seemed to relax. They began to meander around the sidewalk and empty streets like normal cats do. Most of them disappeared into the alleys or around corners.

"Let's just call my parents," Quentin said. "I don't really care if I get in trouble. I just want to go home. My cell phone is in my saddlebag. Come on."

Reese nodded. The boys cautiously headed for their bikes, which were on the ground in front of the pizza shop doors.

The sun was quite low now. Quentin dug through his saddlebag and found his phone. "Wow, it's after six," he said, checking the display screen. "No wonder you're so hungry."

"Yup, it's time for dinner," Reese said. "Just call your parents so we can get out of here. I hope they know where this weird town is."

Reese nodded, tapped some buttons on his cell, and put the phone to his ear. It beeped loudly twice. "No signal," Reese said, looking at the phone's display. "Let's walk till I can get a few bars."

The boys walked their bikes right down the middle of Main Street. The only car they had seen moving was Carol's, so they weren't concerned about traffic. They were more worried about the dark alleys near the sidewalks and buildings than they were about cars.

After a few minutes, a handful of cats began to appear on the sidewalks. They lined up around the two boys on both sides. Then a few more crept into sight, walking along the tops of the nearby wood fences. They seemed to follow the boys as they walked.

Soon, there were dozens of cats of every color. All of the them were ragged and feral. They were staring at Quentin and Reese.

"I've never seen so many stray cats," Quentin said.

Reese shivered. "This is the creepiest town ever," he said.

Chapter 5: Nightfall

The boys finally reached the end of the business area of town and crossed onto a quiet residential street.

Quentin looked down the row of small two-story homes. He spotted a little green car parked in a driveway at the end of the block. "Look," he said. He pointed down the side street. "That's the pizza woman's car."

Reese nodded. "Maybe she'll let us into the bike shop," he said. "Come on."

Reese and Quentin started down the block. The trees on the side street were tall and thick. With the sun nearly set, the air had a fresh chill. A soft orange light filtered through the leaves, casting trembling shadows across the cars and sidewalks.

As the boys started down the quiet, darkening lane, the cats seemed to vanish. Not a single cat prowled along the sidewalk or walked on top of the fences.

Sometimes Quentin thought he saw something move out of the corner of his eye. But when he turned to look, there was nothing but a skittering leaf in the breeze, or the garbage can lid next to someone's garage.

"Hey, Reese," Quentin said quietly, keeping his eye out for strays. "Remind me to thank you for suggesting this route."

"Very funny," Reese said. "It's not my fault. My brother Jake didn't mention anything about a horde of evil cats!"

Quentin wasn't listening. His eyes scanned the neighborhood nervously. "Do you notice anything weird about these homes?" Quentin asked as they walked.

Reese looked around. "You mean how they all seem . . . empty?" he said.

"More like deserted," Quentin said. All the small houses on the block looked like they had once been nice little homes. But now they were falling apart.

They passed a little gray house. All of its windows were broken and boarded up. The paint was peeling, and the shrubs were either overgrown or simply dead and brown. The other houses on the block were the same.

Finally, Quentin and Reese reached the green car. It was parked in the driveway of a small house. The home looked just like the other houses on the street, except that this one was still in good shape. It was brightly painted in red and yellow, and the shrubs and trees on the property were groomed and green. Daisies bloomed in two boxes under the front windows.

"This must be Carol's house," Quentin said. "Finally. She must be the only thing in this town that isn't creepy."

The boys walked up the gravel path toward the front door. But just as Quentin's foot crunched on the pebbles, the black cat slithered out from behind a shrub. It climbed the front steps and stared at Quentin.

"What the heck!" Quentin said. "It's that same cat again."

"That's not all," Reese said. He tugged Quentin's shirt. "Look behind us."

Quentin had never seen so many cats in his entire life. There were waves of them moving toward their location. Dozens and dozens of them had already gathered at the foot of the driveway, and more were joining the pack.

They began to slowly surround the boys. Their hisses and mews were deafening.

There was no escape.

"We need to run," Quentin said.

"Definitely," Reese said. "Which way?"

Hundreds of cats, all of them dirty and ragged, were encircling the boys. Only a small gap in the wall of fur and claws remained visible.

"Through there," Quentin said. "Now!"

The boys raced through the narrow space. The cats hissed and leapt at the boys as they ran, scratching at their legs.

When the boys reached the next corner, the cats were in front of them, blocking their path once again.

"We're trapped!" Reese blurted out.

"No!" Quentin said. "This way!"

Quentin and Reese rushed through the thinnest part of the pack of cats. As they dashed through, the cats closed behind them like a great door of fur and teeth and claws. The cats hissed and snarled loudly as they chased after the boys. Quentin and Reese were fast, but the cats were getting closer by the second.

As they ran, they entered a dark and desolate street. Any sign of the sun was gone, and a big silver moon loomed low in the sky. There were no houses here — only a deep woods on one side.

On the other side was a great black iron fence. Dark green ivy grew up behind it, hiding whatever lay beyond.

"Quentin," Reese said as he ran, gasping for air. "I have to stop!"

"We have to keep running," Quentin said. "There are too many of them. They're going to kill us!"

Quentin pumped his legs as hard as he could. But no matter how fast he tried to run, he felt like his legs were wrapped in concrete. As his feet pounded the pavement, the cuts in his legs pulsed with pain. When he looked down at his shins, his eyes went wide. His legs were covered with gashes. Blood was turning the top of his white socks red.

A lone black cat swiped at Quentin's shoe. He looked up again and forced himself to run even faster.

However, there wasn't any room left to run. Just a hundred yards down the dark and desolate street, the road ended in a cul-de-sac.

Quentin threw a glance at Reese. "What now?" he yelled, afraid to stop.

Reese came to a sudden halt. Quentin stomped to a stop, as well. The gang of cats had somehow gotten in front of them again.

The mangy creatures prowled and hissed. A few slowly edged toward the boys, as if preparing to attack them.

Reese glanced over his shoulder. "They're behind us, too," he whispered. "We're completely trapped now."

Quentin looked around in desperation. On one side of the road was the dark, thick forest.

Quentin could only guess what wild animals lived in there, and he knew he and Reese wouldn't be able to run through all that brush.

On the other side of the road, there was a break in the black iron fence: a big ornate gate. It was decorated with gargoyles and had the words RAVENS PASS CEMETERY engraved over the entrance.

"We can go into the woods," Quentin said, "or through the gates."

"I'm not going into the woods," Reese said. He shoved Quentin toward the gate. "This way."

"The cemetery?!" Quentin said, shocked. He shoved Reese back. "No way. Don't you see? The cats guided us here. They want us in the cemetery!"

"It's safer than the woods!" Reese shouted. "I'll take imaginary ghosts over bloodthirsty cats any day!"

But they didn't have to decide. The sound of a revving engine came blasting down the dark street.

The little car's headlights flashed across the boys and the cats. Right away, the cats began to scatter.

Most of the cats ran toward the cemetery gates. They squirmed and squeezed themselves between the tight gate bars. A few of the strays, however, remained. They hissed angrily at the car as it approached. Their eyes flashed like fierce little spotlights in the night.

With a great screeching of rubber and brakes, the car skidded to a stop next to the boys, scattering the remaining cats.

The passenger side door of the car flew open. Carol, the woman from the pizza shop, poked her head out the driver's side window and screamed to them, "Get in!"

- Chapter 7: Safe House -

The boys didn't think twice. Quentin dove into the front seat and Reese jumped in after him. The car was already screaming back down the dark street before they could even close the door.

"They're chasing us!" Quentin said, twisting in his seat to look out the back window.

A skinny black cat leapt onto the roof of the car.

The strange cat's claws scraped across the metal with a deafening whine. It arched its back and hissed.

Another cat, this one tan and bloody, dove onto the windshield. The boys screamed. The woman barely flinched.

"I'm Carol Fellino," the woman said. "I saw you boys outside the pizza place earlier. I knew I'd need to find you once the sun was down. I arrived just in time, too. Those mangy cats nearly had you in their cemetery."

"Their cemetery?" Quentin repeated. "So they were herding us!"

Carol nodded. "Exactly," she said.

"What's going on here, anyway?" Reese asked. "What's with all the cats? What kind of crazy town is this?"

She just shook her head. "Too many questions," she said, "and too much to explain. I'll tell you everything when we get back to my house. When we're safe."

Carol sped through the streets back toward her house, swerving around the cats as they ran at her car. The cats didn't seem concerned for their safety. They kept diving at the car, sacrificing themselves to just scratch at the paint or swipe at the tires.

"Why are you being so careful?" Reese asked. "Just plow through them. They're evil cats!"

Carol didn't answer. She just kept driving. Before long, the car came to a jerky stop in her driveway. "Inside," Carol snapped as she jumped from the car. "Now!"

The boys followed as quickly as they could. As soon as they were both inside, she slammed the door behind them.

Without glancing at the boys, Carol walked toward the back of the little house. "Your bikes are in the workshop already," she said. "I'll have that rim fixed for you in a few minutes." She disappeared through a swinging door.

"Thanks," Quentin called after her.

Reese glanced at Quentin. "Where's she going?" he asked. Quentin shrugged.

The woman returned to the room with a pizza box in her hands. "But first things first, I brought you boys a pizza."

Reese's mouth fell open. His stomach grumbled loud enough for Quentin and Carol to hear.

"Thank you so much," Quentin said. "But we really do need to get going. We should have been home hours ago. My parents are going to kill me."

Reese looked at Quentin like he was nuts. "Dude, I'm starving," Reese whispered. "Can't we eat first?"

"Oh, come on," the woman said. She put the box on the table and opened it up. Steam wafted across the room. The smell was overpowering and tempting. "You boys must have been cycling all day. You'll never make it home on an empty stomach."

"We have a few minutes," Reese said. He elbowed Quentin lightly.

"Ow," Quentin said. "Yeah, okay. We can eat a little." He forced a smile at Carol. Then he sat down at the table and pulled a slice from the box.

Carol put plates in front of both boys, along with napkins and forks. Then she poured them each a tall glass of lemonade. Finally, she pulled up a third chair. She sat down with them and sipped from her lemonade.

Quentin took a big bite of pizza. It was delicious. The crust was crisp. The salty pepperoni tasted perfect after a day of sweating. The tomatoes and cheese were so fresh, and the herbs gave it a great flavor.

An odd flavor, Quentin thought, *but still really good.*

"So," Reese said through a mouthful of pizza, "what's with this crazy town?"

"Crazy town?" Carol repeated through clenched teeth. "This is Ravens Pass. It's my home. I've lived here all my life."

"In fact," Carol added, "my family is one of the oldest families in Ravens Pass. We've been here for . . . well, forever."

"He didn't mean anything against the town," Quentin said. "He just meant those cats."

"They tried to kill us," Reese said, nodding.

Carol laughed as she poured herself more lemonade. "Nonsense," she said.

"What?!" Quentin said. "You saw them outside the cemetery! They were attacking your car!"

Carol just shrugged. "Have another slice of pizza, both of you," she said. "It'll just go to waste if you don't."

The boys each took a second slice. "Thanks a lot," Reese said. "It's delicious."

"You're welcome," Carol said. She took a sip of her lemonade. "Anyway, the poor kitties. They thought maybe they could get the two of you into the cemetery."

Reese shivered. "Creepy," he said. "I guess you were right, Quentin. They were trying to herd us into the cemetery, just like you said."

Quentin imagined what would have happened if he and Reese had gone into the cemetery. They would've been trapped behind the big black fence with hundreds of cats waiting for them in the darkness, tearing at them with their claws and teeth.

"Did they . . . ," Quentin began, gulping. "Did they want to eat us?"

Carol put down her lemonade and stared at Quentin. Then she looked at Reese. An eerie grin slowly began to spread across her face.

Finally, Carol covered her mouth and began to chuckle. Then she threw her head back and howled out laughter.

"Eat you?" she said after a few moments. "You two are pretty stupid, aren't you?"

"What?" Quentin asked, confused. That only made Carol laugh again.

Carol got up from the table and went to the closet. She took out a pair of heavy, long gloves.

"Those cats weren't trying to kill you," Carol said. "And they didn't want to eat you."

"But they're not normal," Reese said.

Carol nodded. She pulled on the gloves. "They're certainly not normal," she said. "They're . . . well, they're my children."

"Your children?" Quentin repeated.

"In a way," she said. "I love each and every one of them. I love all cats. They hate me, though. And who can blame them." From the same closet, she pulled out a cat cage and placed it on the floor near the table.

"If they didn't want to kill us," Quentin said, putting down his pizza, "why did they want us to go into the cemetery?"

Carol tapped her chin. "Well, that's what's troubling me," she said. "How did they know you two boys were coming through town?"

"What do you mean?" Quentin asked.

"That black one," she said. "I think he must be their leader. But the point is, they reached you before I could. They must be getting smarter."

"You mean they've attacked people before?" Quentin asked.

"Attacked?" Carol repeated. "Boy, aren't you listening? They didn't attack you. They tried to save you."

"Save us?" Quentin asked. "Save us from what, exactly?"

"From me, obviously," Carol said. "I hate the cemetery. The women of my family can't set foot in there without panicking or fainting. You would've been safe there."

"You . . . ," Quentin said. He quickly stood up. His chair fell backward. "What *are* you?!"

Reese stopped eating. He held the slice of pizza held halfway between his mouth and his plate. "What's wrong, Q?" he finally asked.

Quentin's eyes went wide. He turned his head toward Reese without taking his eyes off Carol. He whispered to Reese, "We have to get out of here!"

Quentin grabbed Reese by the shoulder. "Come on!" he said, pulling Reese toward the door.

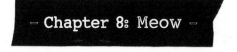

Chapter 8: Meow

Carol didn't bother to chase them. She just sat back down and took a sip of her drink. "It's really too bad the cats can't speak," she said.

Quentin grabbed the doorknob, but it wouldn't budge. "It's locked," he said. Then he spun to face Carol again. "Let us go, you crazy cat lady!"

"Where would you go?" Carol asked. "As I was saying, it's a shame they couldn't simply talk to you. Of course, they used to speak all the time!"

"The cats?" Reese asked. He slowly walked back toward the table, yelping when he bumped into it.

Carol smirked. "Of course," she said. "They spoke, screamed, shouted, cried . . . when they were still boys."

"Boys . . . ?" Quentin whispered.

Carol nodded again. "So loud and obnoxious," she said. "Now they're quiet. Now they're my most favorite precious animals — cats."

Quentin's hands and arms began to itch. He looked down at them and felt his stomach tie itself into knots.

Quentin's hands had curled and twisted toward his elbows, as if they were folding themselves in half. Thick patches of hair had begun to sprout along his arms like little furry spots.

"I adore cats," Carol said, eyeing Quentin intensely. "They're so quiet and graceful."

Quentin was panicking now. He closed his eyes tightly. *It's all just a bad dream,* he told himself.

Quentin raised his hand to his face to pinch himself. But instead of fingers, he felt fur tickle his cheek. Quentin opened his eyes to see that he no longer had fingers at all. Little furry nubs had taken their place.

Sharp claws began to painfully poke their way through the little furry paws that used to be his hands.

"Oh, my kitties never stay with me very long," Carol said. "But I don't mind. There will always be another cat . . . or two."

Quentin's bones crunched and curled and shrank. His legs twisted inward, forcing him to his knees. The pain was overwhelming.

Quentin opened his mouth to scream, but nothing came out. The world around him seemed to be growing larger. He felt small, helpless, and cold.

On all fours, Quentin struggled to stand, but his legs just wouldn't lift him. The kitchen table seemed to be miles above his head.

He looked for Reese, but didn't see him. He just saw a gray cat cowering under the kitchen table, hissing and baring its teeth.

Again, Quentin tried to scream. But only a soft "meow" escaped from his lips. He felt a gloved hand grasp him under his furry belly. Carol scooped him into the cat carrier and closed the door behind him.

"There, there," the woman whispered, close to his ear. "That's a good kitty."

Case number: 232328

Date reported: September 17

Local police: None

Victims: Quentin Sparks, age 14; Reese Michaels, age 13; several other missing kids

Civilian witnesses: None

Disturbance: Two students were reported missing. Mr. and Mrs. Sparks, parents of one of the missing boys, came to me after the police failed to find any leads.

Evidence: A strange stray cat appeared on the Sparks' doorstep the other night carrying a scrap of paper in its mouth, refusing to leave.

Suspect information: Carol Fellino, age 36

CASE NOTES:

THE SCRAP OF PAPER THE CAT WAS CARRYING TURNED
OUT TO BE A UTILITY BILL FOR ONE CAROL FELLINO, A
LOCAL RESIDENT OF RAVENS PASS. IT WASN'T MUCH TO
GO ON, BUT IT WAS THE ONLY LEAD I HAD.

WHEN I ARRIVED AT THE FELLINO RESIDENCE, THE
PREMISES WERE CRAWLING WITH CATS. MS. FELLINO
INVITED ME IN, CAREFUL NOT TO LET ANY OF THEM
INSIDE. SHE WAS QUITE COOPERATIVE IN ANSWERING
QUESTIONS, AND OFFERED ME A SLICE OF PIZZA FRESH
FROM HER OVEN. I RAISED THE SLICE TO MY MOUTH
AND IMMEDIATELY NOTED THE SCENT OF BELLADONNA,
A RARE HERB. ANY WITCHCRAFT EXPERT KNOWS ABOUT
THE TRANSFORMATIVE EFFECTS OF BELLADONNA. I
POINTED AT HER HERB GARDEN BY THE WINDOW, ASKING
HER IF SHE OFTEN USED IT IN ANY OF HER RECIPES.

IMMEDIATELY, SHE RAN OUT THE DOOR. BEFORE I COULD
GIVE CHASE, THE CATS OUTSIDE SWARMED UPON HER,
HISSING AND SCRATCHING HER, UNTIL SHE FELL TO THE
GROUND. FROM THAT POINT, IT WAS A SIMPLE MATTER
OF REVERSING THE HERB'S EFFECTS BY FEEDING THE
CATS SOME WOLFSBANE. AN HOUR LATER, MS. FELLINO
WAS BEHIND BARS, AND TWENTY-THREE FAMILIES HAD
THEIR KIDS BACK.

DEAR READER,

THEY ASKED ME TO WRITE ABOUT MYSELF. THE FIRST THING YOU NEED TO KNOW IS THAT JASON STRANGE IS NOT MY REAL NAME. IT'S A NAME I'VE TAKEN TO HIDE MY TRUE IDENTITY AND PROTECT THE PEOPLE I CARE ABOUT.

YOU WOULDN'T BELIEVE THE THINGS I'VE SEEN, WHAT I'VE WITNESSED. IF PEOPLE KNEW I WAS TELLING THESE STORIES, SHARING THEM WITH THE WORLD, THEY'D TRY TO GET ME TO STOP. BUT THESE STORIES NEED TO BE TOLD, AND I'M THE ONLY ONE WHO CAN TELL THEM.

I CAN'T TELL YOU MANY DETAILS ABOUT MY LIFE. I CAN TELL YOU I WAS BORN IN A SMALL TOWN AND LIVE IN ONE STILL. I CAN TELL YOU I WAS A POLICE DETECTIVE HERE FOR TWENTY-FIVE YEARS BEFORE I RETIRED. I CAN TELL YOU I'M STILL OUT THERE EVERY DAY AND THAT CRAZY THINGS ARE STILL HAPPENING.

I'LL LEAVE YOU WITH ONE QUESTION—IS ANY OF THIS TRUE?

JASON STRANGE
RAVENS PASS

Glossary

bounded (BOUND-id)—moved forward quickly with leaps and jumps

deserted (di-ZHURT-id)—abandoned

desolate (DESS-uh-luht)—empty or uninhabited

feline (FEE-line)—to do with cats, or cat-like

feral (FAIR-uhl)—like a wild animal

horde (HORD)—a large, noisy, moving crowd of people or animals

mangy (MAYN-gee)—shabby or rough looking

pounced (POUNSSD)—jumped on something and grabbed hold of it

slinking (SLINGK-ing)—moving slowly and sneakily

skittering (SKIT-er-ing)—running lightly or rapidly

tensed (TENSSD)—grew tight and stiff in anticipation or preparation

wicked (WIK-id)—cruel or evil

1. Some people believe that crossing paths
   with a black cat is bad luck. Do you
   believe in any superstitions? Why or
   why not?

2. What was the scariest part of this book?
   Why?

3. Reese and Quentin are transformed into
   cats. If you had to be transformed into
   an animal, what animal would you
   choose?

WRITING PROMPTS

1. If you were trapped in a town filled with feral cats, how would you escape? Write about it.

2. Imagine the last chapter of this book from Carol's perspective. Why is she turning the boys into cats? Rewrite the last chapter of this book from Carol's point of view.

3. Reese and Quentin get lost in a strange town. Have you ever gotten lost? What happened? Write about it.